W9-AKS-352

Grateful acknowledgment is made to the following for permission to reprint previously published material:

Addison-Wesley Publishing Company for "Little Donkey Close Your Eyes" by Margaret Wise Brown from NIBBLE, NIBBLE. Copyright © 1959 by William R. Scott. A Young Scott Book. Reprinted by permission of Addison-Wesley, Reading, Massachusetts.

Atheneum Publishers, Inc., for "Waking" by Lilian Moore from I FEEL THE SAME WAY. Copyright © 1967 by Lilian Moore. Reprinted by permission of Atheneum Publishers.

Patricia Ayres for "Pretending" by Bobbi Katz. Copyright © 1973 by Bobbi Katz. Reprinted by permission of the author.

Basil Blackwell Publisher for "The Happy Sheep" by Wilfred Thorley. Reprinted by permission of Basil Blackwell Publisher, Oxford.

Marchette Chute for "Going to Bed" from AROUND AND ABOUT. Copyright © 1957 by E.P. Dutton. Reprinted by permission of the author.

E.P. Dutton & Co., Inc., for "Vespers" by A.A. Milne from WHEN WE WERE VERY YOUNG. Copyright 1924 by E.P. Dutton, Co.; renewed © 1952 by A.A. Milne. Reprinted by permission of the publisher, E.P. Dutton, Inc. Canadian rights administered by McClelland and Stewart Limited. British rights administered by Associated Book Publishers Ltd.

Aileen Fisher for "After a Bath" from UP THE WINDY HILL (New York: Abelard, 1953). Copyright renewed 1981. "Who's Sleepy?" from I WONDER HOW, I WONDER WHY (New York: Abelard-Schuman, 1962). Reprinted by permission of the author.

Harcourt Brace Jovanovich, Inc., for "Keep a Poem in Your Pocket" by Beatrice Schenk de Regniers from SOMETHING SPECIAL. Reprinted by permission of the publisher.

Michael Patrick Hearn for "Naming Sheep." Copyright © 1981 by Michael Patrick Hearn. Reprinted by permission of the author.

Holt, Rinehart and Winston, Publishers, for "How Far?" by Leland B. Jacobs from IS SOMEWHERE ALWAYS FAR AWAY? Copyright © 1967 by Leland B. Jacobs. Reprinted by permission of Holt, Rinehart and Winston, Publishers.

Philomel Books for "All Tucked In" by Clyde Watson from CATCH ME & KISS ME & SAY IT AGAIN. Text copyright © 1978 by Clyde Watson. Reprinted by permission of Philomel Books, a Division of The Putnam Publishing Group. British rights administered by Curtis Brown, Ltd.

Russell & Volkening, Inc., for "Night" by Mary Ann Hoberman. Copyright © 1959 by Mary Ann Hoberman. Reprinted by permission of Russell & Volkening as agents for the author.

Weekly Reader Books offers several exciting card and activity programs.
For information, write to WEEKLY READER BOOKS, P.O. Box 16636, Columbus, Ohio 43216.

The Evening Is Coming

The evening is coming.
The sun sinks to rest.
The birds are all flying
Straight home to their nests.
"Caw, caw," says the crow
As he flies overhead.
It's time little children
Were going to bed.

Here comes the pony.
His work is all done.
Down through the meadow
He takes a good run.
Up go his heels,
And down goes his head.
It's time little children
Were going to bed.

—Anonymous

Going to Bed

I'm always told to hurry up—
   Which I'd be glad to do,
If there were not so many things
   That need attending to.

But first I have to find my towel
   Which fell behind the rack,
And when a pillow's thrown at me
   I have to throw it back.

And then I have to get the things
   I need in bed with me.
Like marbles and my birthday train
   And Pete the chimpanzee.

I have to see my polliwog
   Is safely in its pan,
And stand a minute on my head
   To be quite sure I can.

I have to bounce upon my bed
　　To see if it will sink,
And then when I am covered up
　　I find I need a drink.

—Marchette Chute

Who's Sleepy?

Who's sleepy?
Not me.
Who's sleepy?
Not *I*.
Not the owl in the tree,
the stars in the sky,
the bat on the wing,
the cat on the prowl,
the frog near the spring,
the dog with a howl.

Not the sickle of moon,
the trickle of water,
the skunk, the raccoon,
the mouse and her daughter.

Who's sleepy?
Not deer.
Not crickets I hear.
Not rabbits and such.
Not me...
       very much.

—*Aileen Fisher*

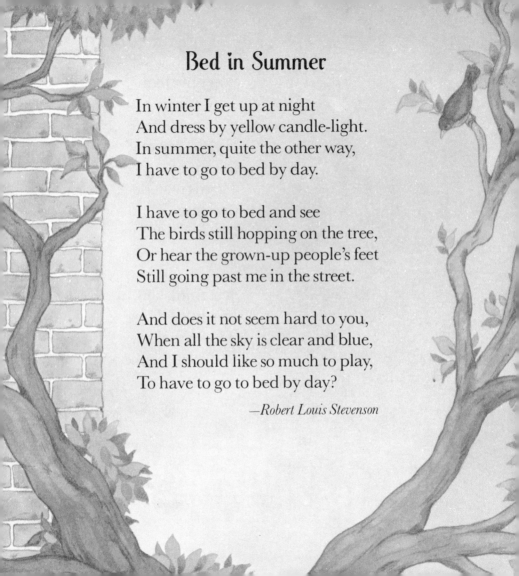

Bed in Summer

In winter I get up at night
And dress by yellow candle-light.
In summer, quite the other way,
I have to go to bed by day.

I have to go to bed and see
The birds still hopping on the tree,
Or hear the grown-up people's feet
Still going past me in the street.

And does it not seem hard to you,
When all the sky is clear and blue,
And I should like so much to play,
To have to go to bed by day?

—*Robert Louis Stevenson*

After a Bath

After my bath
I try, try, try
to wipe myself
till I'm dry, dry, dry.

Hands to wipe
and fingers and toes
and two wet legs
and a shiny nose.

Just think how much
less time I'd take
if I were a dog
and could shake, shake, shake.

—*Aileen Fisher*

The Man in the Moon

The Man in the Moon looked out of the moon,
Looked out of the moon and said,
" 'Tis time for all children on the earth
To think about getting to bed!"

—Anonymous

Night

The night is coming softly, slowly;
Look, it's getting hard to see.
    Through the windows,
    Through the door,
    Pussyfooting
    On the floor,
    Dragging shadows,
    Crawling,
    Creeping,
    Soon it will be time for sleeping.
Pull down the shades.
Turn on the light.
Let's pretend it isn't night.

—Mary Ann Hoberman

The Star

Twinkle, twinkle, little star,
How I wonder what you are!
Up above the world so high,
Like a diamond in the sky.

—Jane Taylor

Willie Winkie

Wee Willie Winkie runs through the town,
Upstairs and downstairs in his nightgown,
Rapping at the window, crying through the lock,
Are the children all in bed, for now it's eight o'clock?

—Anonymous

Vespers

Little Boy kneels at the foot of the bed,
Droops on the little hands little gold head.
Hush! Hush! Whisper who dares!
Christopher Robin is saying his prayers.

God bless Mummy. I know that's right.
Wasn't it fun in the bath tonight?
The cold's so cold, and the hot's so hot.
Oh! *God bless Daddy*—I quite forgot.

If I open my fingers a little bit more,
I can see Nanny's dressing-gown on the door.
It's a beautiful blue, but it hasn't a hood.
Oh! *God bless Nanny and make her good.*

Mine has a hood, and I lie in bed,
And pull the hood right over my head,
And I shut my eyes, and I curl up small,
And nobody knows that I'm there at all.

Oh! *Thank you, God, for a lovely day.*
And what was the other I had to say?
I said "Bless Daddy," so what can it be?
Oh! Now I remember. *God bless me.*

Little Boy kneels at the foot of the bed,
Droops on the little hands little gold head.
Hush! Hush! Whisper who dares!
Christopher Robin is saying his prayers.

—*A. A. Milne*

All Tucked In

All tucked in & roasty toasty
Blow me a kiss good-night
Close your eyes till morning comes
Happy dreams & sleep tight

—Clyde Watson

Keep a Poem in Your Pocket

Keep a poem in your pocket
and a picture in your head
and you'll never feel lonely
at night when you're in bed.

The little poem will sing to you
the little picture bring to you
a dozen dreams to dance to you
at night when you're in bed.

So—
Keep a picture in your pocket
and a poem in your head
and you'll never feel lonely
at night when you're in bed.

—Beatrice Schenk de Regniers

Hush, Little Baby

Hush, little baby, don't say a word,
Mama's going to buy you a mockingbird.

And if that mockingbird don't sing,
Mama's going to buy you a diamond ring.

And if that diamond ring turns brass,
Mama's going to buy you a looking glass.

And if that looking glass gets broke,
Mama's going to buy you a billy goat.

And if that billy goat won't pull,
Mama's going to buy you a cart and bull.

And if that cart and bull turn over,
Mama's going to buy you a dog named Rover.

And if that dog named Rover won't bark,
Mama's going to buy you a horse and cart.

And if that horse and cart fall down,
You'll still be the sweetest little baby in town.

—Anonymous

Little Donkey Close Your Eyes

Little Donkey on the hill
Standing there so very still
Making faces at the skies
Little Donkey close your eyes.

Little Monkey in the tree
Swinging there so merrily
Throwing cocoanuts at the skies
Little Monkey close your eyes.

Little Pig that squeals about
Make no noises with your snout
No more squealing to the skies
Little Pig now close your eyes.

Wild young birds that sweetly sing
Curve your heads beneath your wing
Dark night covers all the skies
Wild young birds now close your eyes.

Weekly Reader Children's Book Club presents

Care Bears
Book of Bedtime Poems

selected by Bobbi Katz • illustrated by Dora Leder

A Care Bear™ Book from Random House, New York

Original Title: Bedtime Bear's Book of Bedtime Poems.

Copyright © 1983 by American Greetings Corporation. Care Bear and Care Bears are trademarks of American Greetings Corporation. All rights reserved under International and Pan-American Copyright Conventions. Published in the United States by Random House, Inc., New York, and simultaneously in Canada by Random House of Canada Limited, Toronto. *Library of Congress Cataloging in Publication Data:* Main entry under title: Bedtime bear's book of bedtime poems. "A Care Bear book from Random House, New York." SUMMARY: Twenty lullabies and other bedtime poems by Robert Louis Stevenson, A. A. Milne, Aileen Fisher, and other English, American, and anonymous authors. 1. Lullabies. 2. Sleep—Juvenile poetry. 3. Children's poetry, English. 4. Children's poetry, American. [1. Lullabies. 2. Bedtime—Poetry. 3. English poetry—Collections. 4. American poetry—Collections] I. Katz, Bobbi. II. Leder, Dora, ill. PR1195.L8B42 1983 821'.008'00354 83-3162 ISBN: 0-394-85956-1 (trade); 0-394-95956-6 (lib. bdg.) Manufactured in the United States of America 1 2 3 4 5 6 7 8 9 0 This book is a presentation of **Weekly Reader Children's Book Club.** Weekly Reader Children's Book Club offers book clubs for children from preschool through junior high school. For further information write to: **Weekly Reader Children's Book Club** 4343 Equity Drive, Columbus, Ohio 43228

A Visitor

When suppertime is over,
When your toys are put away,
When you've sailed ships in the bathtub,
When you can't go out and play;
When you're wearing your pajamas,
When you're neatly tucked in bed,
When you've had some milk and crackers,
When the last good-night is said;
When someone's turned your light out,
When no one else is there;
That's exactly when I'll visit—
My name is Bedtime Bear!

—Bedtime Bear

Old black cat down in the barn
Keeping five small kittens warm
Let the wind blow in the skies
Dear old black cat close your eyes.

Little child all tucked in bed
Looking such a sleepyhead
Stars are quiet in the skies
Little child now close your eyes.

—Margaret Wise Brown

Pretending

When you are in bed and it's cold outside,
do you ever pretend that you have to hide?
Do you curl up your toes?
Do you wrinkle your nose?
Do you make yourself little so none of you shows?

Do you pull the sheet over the whole of your face
and pretend you are in some faraway place?
Mother thinks you are sleeping,
but she does not know
that all tucked in your bed, you have places to go.

—*Bobbi Katz*

The Happy Sheep

All through the night the happy sheep
Lie in the meadow grass asleep.

Their wool keeps out the frost and rain
Until the sun comes round again.

They have no buttons to undo,
Nor hair to brush like me and you,

And with the light they lift their heads
To find their breakfast on their beds

Or rise and walk about and eat
The carpet underneath their feet.

—Wilfrid Thorley

The Land of Nod

From breakfast on through all the day
At home among my friends I stay;
But every night I go abroad
Afar into the land of Nod.

All by myself I have to go.
With none to tell me what to do—
All alone beside the streams
And up the mountain-sides of dreams.

The strangest things are there for me,
Both things to eat and things to see,
And many frightening sights abroad
Till morning in the land of Nod.

Try as I like to find the way,
I never can get back by day,
Nor can remember plain and clear
The curious music that I hear.

—Robert Louis Stevenson

Naming Sheep

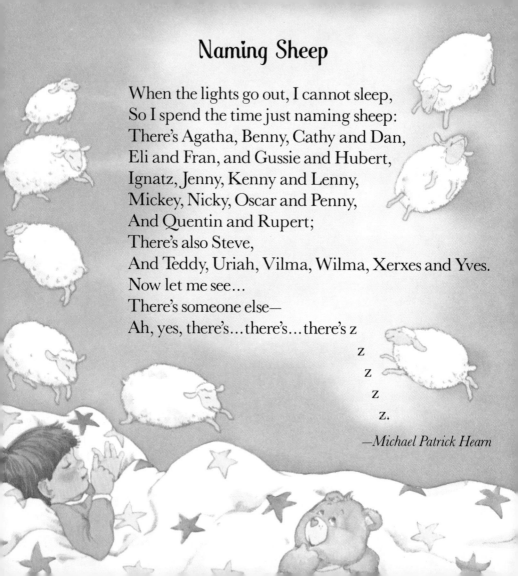

When the lights go out, I cannot sleep,
So I spend the time just naming sheep:
There's Agatha, Benny, Cathy and Dan,
Eli and Fran, and Gussie and Hubert,
Ignatz, Jenny, Kenny and Lenny,
Mickey, Nicky, Oscar and Penny,
And Quentin and Rupert;
There's also Steve,
And Teddy, Uriah, Vilma, Wilma, Xerxes and Yves.
Now let me see…
There's someone else—
Ah, yes, there's…there's…there's z

z

z

z

z.

—*Michael Patrick Hearn*

How Far?

How far is a dream?
　As far as a star
　High in the sky?

How far is a dream?
　At the close of the day
　A dream is just
　A pillow away.

—Leland B. Jacobs

Waking

My secret way of waking
is like a place
to hide.
I'm very still,
my eyes are shut.
They all think I am sleeping
but
I'm wide awake inside.

They all think I am sleeping
but
I'm wiggling my toes.
I feel sun-fingers
on my cheek.
I hear voices whisper-speak.
I squeeze my eyes
to keep them shut
so they will think I'm sleeping
BUT
I'm really wide awake inside
—and no one knows!

—Lilian Moore